the session

I should rather you called me Detective

the session

a novella in dialogue

aaron
petrovich

original
monotypes

vilem
benes

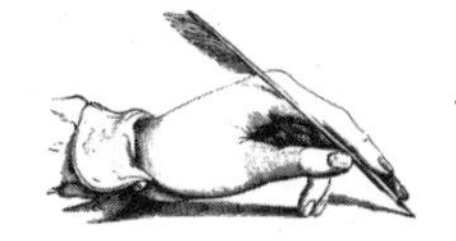

Hotel St. George Press
Brooklyn, New York

The Session is a work of fiction. All names, characters, places and incidents are the product of the author's imagination. Any resemblance to actual events or locales or persons, living or dead, is entirely coincidental.

Portions of *The Session* originally appeared in *Exquisite Corpse* #5&6.

Cover Design by Alex Rose.
Cover Illustration by Vilem Benes.
Author's Portrait by Vilem Benes.

Published by Hotel St. George Press

ISBN 13: 978-0-9789103-0-3

LCCN: 2006936696

First Printing

Hotel St. George Press
*book a room
www.hotelstgeorgepress.com

Dedicated

LJP MVD

Indebted

Alex, David, Johanna, Johnny

What we're after here is the *truth* of the situation.

I've got it.

I'm pleased to hear it.

In the palm of my hands.

That's the wrong place for it.

On the edge of my seat?

In anticipation of . . . ?

. . .

. . . What?

What?

What are you waiting for?

Who says I'm waiting?

You've just done.

I said no such thing.

You are on the edge, young man, of your seat.

But I'm standing.

They're your words.

There are not, even, any seats within this room to sit in.

It's *your* expression.

It's *only* an expression.

Your expressions contain dangerous preconditions.

There are only, between individuals, expressions.

Nonetheless, for what are you on the edge of your seat waiting?

It's a moot point.

I'd like to know. What are you waiting for?

. . . The truth?

See, that's what I'm talking about.

Are you?

You can't lie in waiting for this truth.

Like a snake?

This truth won't come listlessly upon you.

Like the feral field mouse upon the hungry jaws of the bathing snake?

Not this truth, Smith. Not *this* of truth.

I'd rather you didn't call me that.

What?

Smith.

It's your name.

I'm aware of that.

I'm not to call you by name?

You are also called Smith.

I'm aware of that.

I might not know which Smith it is to whom you speak.

When I'm speaking to you, Smith, you'll know it.

Nor *of* which Smith it is you speak. Nor which Smith to speak to. Nor which Smith it is indeed who speaks. Nor, when you are speaking, and we are able to discern that you are speaking, and not I, whether you are speaking to you or to me. Nor whether, and this is perhaps the crux of it, for me, at least: When I am speaking, and we are able, by whatever means, to agree that I am speaking—because I have, in the past, spoken, and we know how I speak—I am speaking to you and not to me. To myself I mean. I don't want it to come to that. I don't want to speak to myself. It's not—sanitary. People who speak to their own selves are not, as a general rule, clean. They carry a certain odor.

Have I ever mistaken you for something else?

The odor they carry is symptomatic of their reintegration with the Earth—with the cycles of growth and decay on the Earth—from what rank and rotting organism they no longer are able to think of themselves as separate.

Have I ever taken you to be anything but what you now are?

If I no longer were able to think of myself as an entity that is separate from the world that surrounds him, I should find myself feeling rather—unable to go on.

We must go on.

I can't go on.

You must.

Have I ever taken you to be anything but what you now are?

I am no longer the primary agent in my own destination.

Just because you have correctly perceived that you are an agent in an already given situation does not preclude you from affecting the situation's outcome.

I am decidedly nothing.

You must be careful not to remove yourself from the equation.

I am the *mathematical absolute* of nothing.

You must be careful not to remove yourself from any equation to which you are the solution.

I am the void described by the outline on the zero in nothing.

You are deceived, I believe, by a beguiling melancholy.

I have seen my life, and it is a big empty nothing in my head that takes up space, though I cannot imagine why.

Despair, however, only comes to he who believes that he's perceived the future.

I make no claims of precognition.

Nor could you. You succumb instead to the *illusion* of a prophetic despair that is developing, over you, qualities of the inevitable.

But I have moved outside a position of self-pity and despair to one of boredom.

Come now, little buddy, I know you better than that.

You don't *know* me well enough to know me.
I know you better, perhaps, than you yourself do.
I don't know how to respond to that.
I knew you would say that.
You're a real piece of work, you know that?
I know, Smith. I know.
I know something you could call me.
I can think of a few things.
I should rather you called me Detective.
It's not your name!
I've earned it!
I'm not denying it.
I completed my courses.
I'm aware of that.
It stands to reason.
I, also, am a detective.
I never thought of that.
How will we know of which detective it is you speak?
This will never do.
Are you talking to me?
I'm not talking to myself.
I thought perhaps that you were.
I'm off track.
Judging from the smell.
I've lost my place.
You were waiting for the truth.
Was I?
On the edge of your seat.

Nonsense.

That's what I'm telling you.

You can't wait for this truth.

This truth won't come suddenly upon you.

Except, perhaps, in a moment of inspiration?

You'll want to rein this truth in.

Hop in the saddle?

Get in the driver's seat!

Grab hold the horns!

Now you've got it!

I believe I do!

Now you've *got* it, let's get back to it.

Let's do that.

Let's go over what we know.

We cannot, after all, know what we do not know until we've covered what we know.

What do we know?

We must, after all, review all we think we know before we know what we cannot.

. . . I'm *asking* you.

What?

What we know.

You don't know?

I'd like to hear it from you.

That's very considerate.

I respect your opinion.

That's not necessary, but thank you.

I understand that it isn't necessary, and I accept your gratitude.

Will you permit me to rephrase the question?

You, also, are entitled to your opinion.

This is a kind thing for you to say. Shall we begin?

Knowing I've your respect, I am, in fact, eager to begin.

What, then, do we know?

He's dead.

Please be thorough: *Who* is dead?

I will try to be more specific: the Mathematician.

Thank you. And what is he missing?

In his position, I would miss the way the window gathers the morning light into a ball and shatters it across the far wall.

. . .

. . .

Will you permit me to rephrase the question?

You've not found my response to your liking?

On the contrary, I have experienced in full the delightful whimsy of your observations, but had intended to take our investigation in less imaginative directions.

I am pleased that you have found whimsy in the simple pleasures of an ordinary man, and will be happy to reconsider the question.

This is both gracious and accommodating, and I will concede that my question was, perhaps, not direct.

Not at all.

Of what, to rephrase the question, has the Mathematician been robbed?

Mortality.

Please be specific.

Mortal doldrums.

I was thinking of something internal.

The everlasting flame?

Something of the person.

Do you believe in the existence of the soul?

Something physical.

Ah. It suddenly occurs to me where you are going with this.

It would please me to hear it.

The Mathematician, who is dead, has been robbed of his bodily organs.

See now, you don't have to say bodily there.

There are organs of all kinds that can be found in many places.

Bodily is implicit.

Organ procurement organizations have organs. Medical research facilities have organs. Certain morgues at certain times have organs. Political journals can be thought of as organs.

Bodily is inferred.

Churches have organs.

I'm aware of that.

It stands to reason.

Let's move beyond the organs.

It's an important point.

I'm not denying it.

It's a savage evisceration.

Now *that's* a fact.

Is it?

Yes.

Then we've reined it in then.

What?

Like you said.

What have we reined in?

The truth.

No. We haven't.

Regarding the organs.

What about the organs?

That they're missing.

That is not a truth.

They're not missing?

It's a fact.

I thought we've just agreed that they are missing.

The fact that they are missing is a *fact*.

Yes!

Not a truth.

No?

Not the kind we're after.

I understand. This truth we seek is not a fact.

No—well—yes—well—not in so many words. No. The truth we seek behaves like a fact—like a complete thing in and of itself—but regardless of our participation in it.

Sometimes, in order to survive, I find that I can not begin to attempt to pretend to comprehend your lessons.

You sell yourself short.

I was not the top of my class.

Nonetheless, you have risen steadily through the ranks.

There were others who seemed seamlessly to grasp what I could scarcely glimpse.

It was your willingness to improve that led me to select you.

A decision, I fear, that you are learning to regret.

Nonsense. I am here to guide you.

I am but a wayward dinghy held from drifting by the guiding light of your beacon.

Permit me to bring you safely to the shore.

You are an illuminating light in a darkening sky, and I am a dirty little dinghy.

The question you must ask yourself is—

Am I not a little dinghy?

Does there exist an aspect to the Mathematician's savage evisceration that remains dependent upon our perceptions of it?

As when a thing is compared to some other thing with such regularity in common practice that it becomes generally accepted as precisely the same as the *other* thing?

I'm afraid I haven't followed you.

Where?

By which I mean to say, to borrow a metaphor, I am adrift in the open seas of your ambiguity.

Ah. Permit me to provide an example.

If you would be so kind.

As, for example, when the word coined to allude to the indefatigable energy-that-connects-everything is used with such regularity in common practice that it becomes generally accepted as the actual source for the energy it once had only alluded to?

. . .

As, in more specific terms, when humanity made God of an inkling?

I am pleased with your progress if not with your preference for parable. There are truths and there are facts and then there are those rarely encountered truths that act on us as though they are facts over which we have no control.

Regardless of our participation in them?

And freed from the constraints of the manner we've used to procure them.

This, then, is an implicit truth?

Not precisely.

Is it, then, an inherent truth?

Not precisely.

Is it not, then, an *essential* truth?

Precisely.

Well that would be consistent, in any case, with the lecture.

What lecture?

A Handbook for the Ideologically Impaired

The lecture I attended.

You attended a lecture?

If a man—any man—is not satisfied with his station, will you condemn him, also, for continuing his education?

My surprise is born not of scorn but of pleasure.

I thought I detected a tone.

No tone intended.

None therefore taken.

What was the subject of this lecture?

I'm not entirely certain that I understood it.

What was it entitled?

An Introduction to the Elusive Precepts of Essencism.

You attended a lecture on Essencism?

I did.

The *Mathematician's* Essencism?

The very same. In which he proposed the formation of a collective of sorts. A collective or a club. Like a masonry. Or a cult. In preparation for the end of days.

But that was his last lecture.

Tragically. Though it was intended to be the first in a series of symposia bound by the moniker, *A Handbook for the Ideologically Impaired.*

And you are aware that this is the same lecture—

The first in a now defunct series of lectures—

Yes, I've got that, thank you, the same lecture after which we believe the entire attendant audience—

Having been granted definitive proof of a finite

future with a particularly brutal projection of concentric and expanding, intersecting circles of holographic light—

That's just it, a finite future, returned, as one and at once to the present—

To the now futile present—

As if in a singular loss of its collective mind—

As though consumed by a force over which it had no control—

And savagely eviscerated the speaker.

Allegedly.

You were there?

I was in the back.

Did you see anything?

I was by the windows.

You didn't see anything.

I was standing, as I have said, in the back by the windows, which were covered by a thick black drape of velvet, perhaps, or perhaps it was merely canvas. During the course of the lecture, there appeared through a rend in the fabric a beguiling slice of bright white light that gave the impression the sun had begun to fall. I saw the light. I stepped into the light. I am easily distracted, if you will recall, by sun-fall, or rise, or by light at fall through a distant aperture in an otherwise impenetrable canvas of clouds—in particular at sun-fall—when one can see the sun for its streaks, when its streaks appear as solids, as a composition, I mean, of particulates, of particulate matter, of the particulate matter that passes into us through a rend in the fabric that composes us. I pressed into the fabric, or perhaps it was merely canvas. I followed the light into its folds. *I am,* I remember thinking at the time, *I am light.* I kept my eyes to the last light. I felt the light fall. I felt night fall. I felt the indefatigable energy-that-connects-everything become—I'm not sure if this is a word—fatigable. I think that that's a word. I was covered in an impenetrable canvas of nightfall. It should come to you as no surprise that I have never felt so alone. It was as though night, falling on me, had fallen on the whole of the world. On what remained of the world. On me. I can think of no better way to say it: I was all that remained of the world. It was not until you arrived with your illuminating sirens and headlights and your illuminating flashlights that I recovered, once again, my senses—my sense of sight, I mean—and returned my attention to the lectern. I extricated myself from the situation, from the, if you will, from the folds in the fabric that compose us, and joined you at the door.

I thought you had arrived with us.

I was already in attendance.

And did it never occur to you that you had not, perhaps, also, lost your mind?

What, like the audience?

Are you not, perhaps, also, out of your mind?

The thought had not occurred to me.

Your path is laid out before you.

Then will you please explain to me why you failed to recognize the relevance of your attendance on our investigation?

The only proper explanation I can provide is a complete admission of my own incompetence.

Look at me, dinghy.

I'm looking.

I am your beacon.

I am blinded, now, by your light.

I expect nothing but the best from you.

Your expectations of me, though dear to me, intimidate me.

Though your path is laid out before you, it will not always describe the straight line or the gentle incline.

I shall attempt to sow the wicker bridge to my destiny over the shallow river and sheer slopes of my future.

Let's move on.

Obstacles be damned, I always say.

Pay attention: Would you kindly review with me your impressions regarding the events at the conclusion of the lecture, when we were joined together at the door?

We found that he was dead.

With all due respect, I will remind you to be specific.

My apologies. The Mathematician was dead.

And what was he missing?

In addition to the morning light, mortality, mortal doldrums, and the everlasting flame, and regardless of whether or not you believe in the existence of the soul, the Mathematician was missing his bodily organs. What?

Never mind. What else?

They were kicking him.

With all due respect.

The *lunatics* were kicking him. And jumping on him. Like monkeys. And picking at his hair.

You're quick to call them lunatics.

We're in a nuthouse, aren't we?

We're not qualified to say.

That we're in a nuthouse?

That they're insane.

Then why are they here?

Who brought them here?

We did.

Why did we bring them here?

It was your idea.

You'd like to blame this on me?

That was not my intention.

You'd like to lay the whole thing on me.

I thought you'd know.

What?

Why we brought them here.

I *do* know.

Why?

Because I am of a higher intelligence.

I will concede your point.

I'd like to take a moment to apologize.

I can't keep pace.

I can see I've allowed myself to get ahead of you.

It's enough to breathe.

I'll summarize.

I'm not worthy.

I'll try to be more sensitive.

You are an example to me.

I should not have taken it for granted.

Not at all.

Do you feel able to continue?

I'd like to try.

Chin up. You were wise to point out that it was I who had brought them here. I brought them here, you understand, not *because* they are insane, but to find out *if* they are insane.

If. *Not* because.

Precisely.

They do seem a touch off the rocker.

You've missed my point.

Coupl'a skeins short of a sweater?

We're not qualified to say.

Grandma left the knitting at home?

Listen to me. Are you a doctor?

I've got a gut feeling.

Have your feelings been accredited?

By whom?

By the Institution.

Who could it be that turns upon the door?

The Institution?

Have your feelings been accredited by the Institution?

I can't say that they have.

Do you have your Certificates?

I've got a gut feeling.

DO YOU HAVE YOUR CERTIFICATES?

I HAVEN'T ANY CERTIFICATES.

THEN YOU ARE NOT QUALIFIED, SMITH, TO SAY!

DON'T CALL ME SMITH!

Quiet. The door.

It's moving.

The knob on the door.

Is turning.

Who could it be?

That turns upon the door?

And enters?

The doctor?

Is it the doctor?

Entering?

The doctor.

Is entering.

Enter the doctor.

Enter, doctor.

Enter.

A moment of your time, if you please. I have welcomed you here with my every courtesy, yes? I have extended you, I believe, in these difficult times, my every hospitality. I have even made available to you this little room, yes?—despite the fullness of the asylum.

Yeah, that's all true.

You know what else is true, Doolitlle? There's nothing so full as a full asylum.

You got that right.

Except perhaps a morgue.

A morgue or a mausoleum.

Or, in fact, a simple grave.

Whereas there is nothing so empty—

Please—

As man's pursuit of meaning in the post-digital era of consumer entitlement.

Please. While I am not averse to engaging in the important philosophical matters of our time, I should prefer at present to focus our focus on the present matter at hand. Would that be, for you, agreeable?

Sure.

Why not.

We are in agreement.

Good. I would remind you, therefore, and would seek confirmation to that effect, that I am without reproach in procuring for you a comforting environ from which your investigation—excuse me—from which you might run your little investigation. Yes?

Is that a question?

Yes.

I'm having difficulty understanding your diction.

Are you understanding the question?

Yes.

And you the question will answer?

Yes.

Yes?

The answer to your question is a resounding yes.

You have been nothing short of saintly in your hospitality.

I like that.

And you also tend the verb at the end of your sentences to put.

I am amused by that.

I find your accent amusing.

Your accent and your mustache.

Your accent, your mustache, and your spectacles.

Though I am not so terribly amused—am I?

No.

By the bounty of your nasal hair.

It's a jungle in there.

You could smell the napalm in the morning if you could smell it.

I see. And are you also finding my patience amusing?

They're funny, yeah.

My *patience*.

If a bit bug-eyed, if you know what I mean.

Little bit round the bend.

On the brink.

But a real laugh-riot, in a sort of daffy sort of duck sort of a way.

I said my *patience.*

Yeah, I heard you the first time, Caligari.

Though I'm a bit surprised to hear you say it.

A man in your position.

These whack-jobs are dependent on you.

They're not playing with a full deck.

Coupl'a Taiwanese short of a sweat shop.

Coupl'a—

Coupl'a carnies short of a freak show.

Coupl'a trapeze short of a proper circus.

They're flying without a safety net, Zhivago.

And yet you find them amusing.

Shameful.

A man in your position.

Are you understanding the difference between my *patience* and my *patients*?

I'm not sure where you are going with this.

Are you not feeling well?

Have you your hand in the pharmaceutical trough been dipping?

It's hard to blame you, though.

What with all the cracker-jacks around here.

These lollipops are dependent on you.

It's shameful, really.

A man in your position.

What we are confronting here is a fundamental disconnect regarding the sounds of words and their meanings. Whereas I have said *patience,* you have heard me to say *patients.* But as it takes a patient mind to mind the patient's mind, they are not my patients but my *patience* you have tried. Yes?

. . . Let's just say yes and get along with it.

Good. It had been my intention to receive, from you, which I have done, a calm and open acknowledgment of my good graces, from which common understanding it was subsequently my intention to remind you, which I now am doing, that this room, in fact, the very arena of your investigation, has become available to you on a single condition. Yes?

Yes.

You will recall for me this condition?

You want me to repeat it for you?

If you please.

Fine, but I've got to tell you, Strangelove, I object to this tone that you've adopted.

You're really wearing on my patience.

Yeah, I mean, it's not as though I am your patient.

Nonetheless, as to the question of your condition, you asked me to—what was the word?

To mind—

Yes, that's just it, to *mind*—

To mind my tone.

And, may I ask, have you?

No.

And you will recall for me why I placed on you this condition?

On account of we are in a nuthouse.

It is not the word I would have used. However, I am finding myself to remind you that our residents have suffered an unusual trauma, a prognostic shock, if you will—a pre-traumatic stress disorder for an event that has not yet occurred. Symptomatic of this disturbance is their consistent belief that they have become removed from themselves. They testify independently that they can see themselves as from outside of themselves. They speak to themselves as from outside of themselves. They are not, however, using the word "I" in reference to themselves. They are using the word "I" instead in reference to objects. They are referring to objects and clinging to objects and are confusing themselves sometimes with the objects they are clinging to. It is not as such themselves to whom they speak—to whom they think they speak—but to any object in the world that surrounds them, any one of which they consider a container as viable a vector for their untenable, unstable spirit as they themselves are, and is subsequently addressed as such. By themselves, I mean. Any object at all. Any water glass, for example. Any body of water. Any window pane or frame. Any stream of any astral light in the evening. Any lamp or lamppost. Any postal worker. Any worker bee. It's all the same. Any scream. Any man's scream. They find in your raised voice an object. In your scream, they find themselves reflected. They open their mouths and become your scream. As your scream recedes, they find themselves reflected, also, in the recession. They slowly recede, as if in imitation of an echo. They listen to themselves recede into the distance. The echo is proof of the void. They become the void you echo in. The echo completes to silence. They open their mouths. They open their mouths as if to scream. But say nothing. They *are* nothing. They are the void described by the outline on the zero in—

Well, that's just—

In nothing.

Isn't that just—

Compelling.

Isn't it?

That's just compelling.

I, for one, would like to thank you, quack—

Thank you, for this most informative lecture.

About the lunatics.

This is a fascinating story you tell.

About the lunatics.

Fascinating, and also, well—

I've got to tell you—

It's got the human touch.

It's a tear-jerker, really.

A heartbreaker.

My heart is aching.

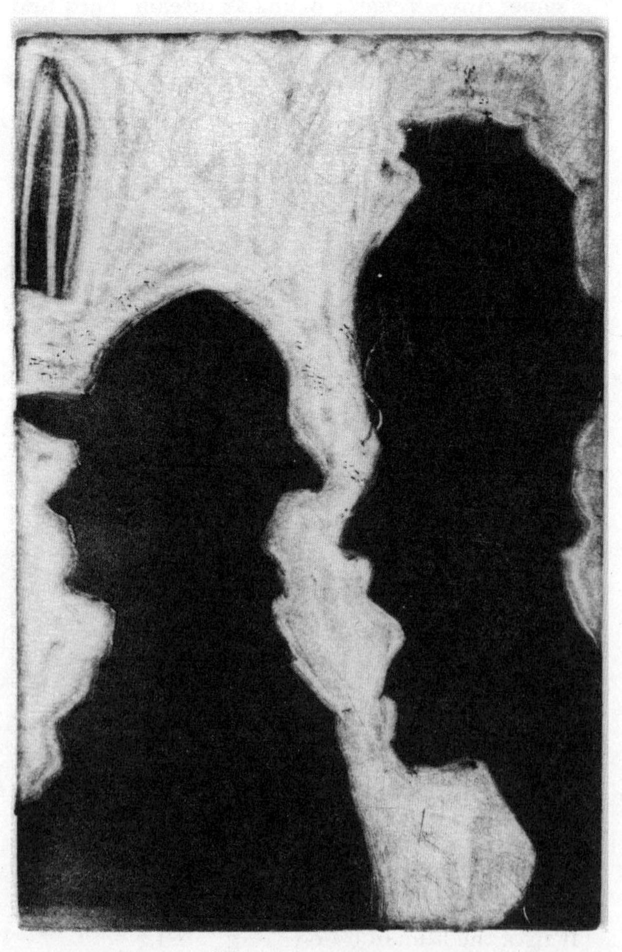

And opened my mouth as if to scream?

And mine also. My heart also aches at this—what's the word?

Injustice.

Yes, at this injustice I have done—

Upon the lunatics—

With my insensitive shouting.

What makes me—

One wonders—

Doesn't one?

At times like these—

What makes a man like me the beast I have become?

Was it a violent upbringing?

An absence of mother's milk?

An excess of mother's milk?

An excess of alienating external media?

The division of labor?

The fundamental misrepresentation of an individual's personal will in a majoritan so-called democracy?

If indeed there is such a thing as personal will in a so-called free economy.

Is personal will a function of the person?

Or of the culture?

Was I a person born for example with will when I came at first from the womb?

And opened my mouth as if to scream?

Or was I immediately infiltrated?

By culture?

Is my personal will nothing more than an umbilical chord?

From culture?

That has wrapped itself around my neck?

An agent?

A double agent?

A symbiont?

A spook?

A domestic spooking program?

A mole?

A burrowing mole?

That has worked its way inside of me?

Pursuant to the needs of culture?

Feeding me and feeding off of me?

Altering me in order to survive by me?

Since the day I was born?

Am I being punished for having been born into culture?

Is being born into culture the same thing as having been born?

It's a question, really, that hasn't any answer.

Though I'll not stop asking it.

Oh, I'll set all my thoughts on it.

I'll not rest tonight.

I'll lie awake all night.

Asking myself this very question.

This life question.

This question that is essential to life.

Life is a question, doctor.

To which no one can provide the answer.
You should know that by now.
Everyone knows that.
It's the Mathematician taught me that.
But not in so many words.
Well, no. Not in so many words. No.
He didn't speak very well.
He didn't really go in for the euphemisms.
Or the expressions.
Like, I don't know—
Like the children are this country's future.
For example.
Or it takes a village to raise a child.
Or—
There is no I in team.
Things like that.
Which is a crock of shit, by the way.
What?
There is no I in team.
Well, of course there isn't any I in team.
The I is in the individual.
Twice.
Three times.
Once in the beginning and twice in the middle.
So what does that tell you about the end?
That's the *real* question.
Everyone knows that.
It's an important lesson.
It's the Mathematician taught me that.

But—

Not in so many words.

Well—no. Not in so many words.

No.

He didn't speak very well.

His ideas cannot be expressed in the language of culture.

His ideas cannot be *reduced* to the language of culture.

His ideas—

Which question the provenance of culture—

Cannot be expressed in the language of culture.

In language, you see, the culture is in the *idea.*

The idea is *not* in the culture.

Consequently.

As I have said.

As you stand here before me.

Judging from the smell.

He didn't speak very well.

But it's the *essence* of the thing that matters.

And an essence, in—well, in its *essence*—

On an essential level, I mean—

Cannot be expressed.

Can it?

Of course not.

Everyone knows that.

You should know that by now, doctor.

It's the Mathematician taught me that.

The Mathematician was an Essencist.

Which is a religion.

Or a philosophy. Or something.

In any case, it's something you can believe in.

And it's something the Mathematician believed in.

And I also, I also believe in this—

This pedagogy.

Or ideology. Or what have you.

Even though its precepts are not accessible to the human mind.

To the cultural mind.

To the mind in culture.

In culture, you see, the culture is in the *mind*.

The mind is *not* in the culture.

The precepts of Essencism, in short, are not accessible to the language of the culture in the mind. Isn't that right?

Of course it's right.

You should know that by now, doctor.

A man in your position.

Everyone knows that.

It's the Mathematician.

It's the Mathematician taught me that.

This is not a system of the mind.

It cannot be articulated.

It cannot be understood.

It can only be accepted.

So there really isn't any need to talk about it, now is there?

The Mathematician's inability to articulate was a demonstration of a profound faith.

None whatsoever.

. . .

The Mathematician's inability to articulate was a demonstration of a profound faith.

. . .

That I cannot express.

. . .

But in the meantime.

To pass the time.

To while the day away.

Until the end of the day.

And into that long night.

I've an investigation to run.

An investigation, incidentally—

That cannot be stayed by the FERAL SENSITIVITIES of a bunch of WRITHING and SEETHING LUNATICS.

Or *residents*, as the good man says.

Very smart to modify that, Smith.

I've asked you not to call me that.

You gonna start that again?

And now I'm asking you again.

I was complimenting you!

Please don't call me Smith!

If I may intercede. While it has been to my benefit, and I believe also to yours, to permit you to explicate your memory of the Mathematician unimpeded, who was, by your solemnity, an important figure for you, and while I should not have wanted to interrupt your soliloquy, it is time, now, to meditate upon what differences have arisen between you in the condition of your bereavement.

What'd he just say?

Might I help you to settle your differences?

You *might.*

I doubt it.

Yeah, but he *might.*

You see how difficult he can be?

He keeps calling me Smith.

You don't like to be called Smith?

No.

And what is your name?

Smith.

. . .

I see. Perhaps we can talk, for a moment, about Smith.

The name or the person?

You see how difficult he can be?

Pardon me. This is my area. Yes?

I know a thing or two about—

Do you have your Certificates?

No.

Good. I am wanting to focus, for the present, on the *name.* Perhaps we can focus on the *person* later.

I'd like that.

Wonderful. What is it about Smith that does not please you?

He is also called Smith.

And this commonality in personas confuses you?

I get confused sometimes. Sometimes, I get upset.

You are being very honest. And why, may I ask, does this upset you?

. . . I'll never be a Smith like him.

Now *that's* a fact.

I am not finding your commentary useful.

I'm just saying—

We are focusing, at present, on Smith.

You gonna let him call you that?

He's trying to help.

I'm beginning to feel quite at home here.

Perhaps we can talk about that later. For now I'd like to ask: Can *you* think of a name you'd like to be called?

I should like to be called Detective.

That's a *nice* name.

I like it.

The gentleman would like to be called Detective.

I, also, am a detective.

I'd like to focus on the matter at hand. Yes?

I find the point relevant.

Is it your intention to sabotage the session?

The session?

Because from my perspective, you are playing the role of the saboteur. Perhaps you can think about that as we close the matter at hand.

I've got an investigation to run.

You're aware of that then?

I've just said.

Then you will agree to use this word, "Detective?"

But he—

Answer the question.

But I—

It's in your best interest. Answer the question.

If it pleases him.

Will it please you?

I'd like that.

Very good. Well. I believe that we've gone far enough for today.

I need to get back to the investigation, anyway.

I understand.

Thank you, doctor.

Please mind your tone.

Good day, doctor.

Perhaps, on another day, now that we've helped to understand your differences, we can begin to focus on what makes you the same.

I can think of nothing in common between us but that we are all merely human.

But it is a start, yes?

It's a fine start, doctor.

It's a thorough waste of time.

Please mind your tone.

Good day, doctor.

Thank you.

Doctor. Good day.

Goodbye.
Good riddance.
Good man.
Don't let the doorknob sodomize you on the way out.
. . .
. . .
Now *that's* a doctor.
Detective.
. . .
Detective.
Are you talking to me?
I'm not talking to myself.
I thought perhaps that you were..
I am calling you "Detective."
It's awfully considerate.
I apologize if I hurt your feelings.
As long as we're understood.
I was trying to make a point.
As long as we're understood.
Shall we proceed?
As long as we're understood.
We were talking about your feelings.
I appreciate that.
Your gut feelings.
Feels nice to get it off the chest.
Your feelings which have not been accredited.
Right.
By the Institution.

Yes.

Are you with me?

No.

I was pointing out that you may have made an errant assumption about whether a lunatic is indeed a lunatic. Is it possible, for example, that your assumption was false?

It's not likely.

Is it possible?

Improbable at best.

But possible.

In the end.

I will ask you to consider the realm of possibilities, in your responses.

I will endeavor to do so.

We cannot attain our truth on false assumptions.

The Detective has recognized your point, and is prepared to continue. What?

Never mind. Did we find any organs?

On whom?

The lunatics.

Oh, they're lunatics now, are they?

For the sake of argument.

If it pleases you.

Did they have any organs?

I should think they did.

You didn't tell me.

I thought you knew.

Where are they?

What?

The organs. Where are the organs?

I'm not a doctor.

Permit me to rephrase.

By all means.

Did they have the Mathematician's organs?

They did not.

Have we recovered the Mathematician's organs?

We have not.

Is it possible that the motive for the Mathematician's murder was toward the unlawful possession of his viscera?

It's possible.

By one of our underground organ procurement organizations?

They might have eaten them.

This is an interesting point you make.

We'll want to perform an autopsy.

On whom?

The lunatics.

They're not dead.

When they're dead.

Were you planning to kill them?

The thought had not occurred to me.

Then an autopsy is out of the question.

I wouldn't be opposed to it.

What?

Killing them.

This is not an option.

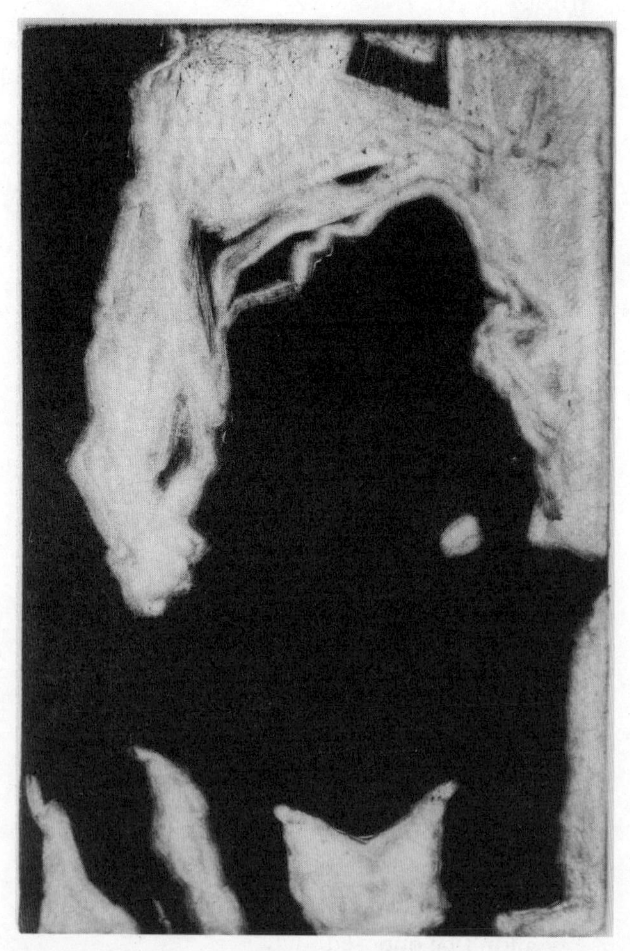

It would be possible, I think, to hang myself by these frames.

If it were, I mean.

It isn't.

You can count on me.

It won't be necessary.

Even so.

It's not necessary.

Not necessary. But *possible*.

. . .

. . .

It would be possible, I think, to hang myself by these frames.

Well, yes, but you'd want a length of rope. Or a belt. A big belt. Like, a sumo belt. Only, you wouldn't want to block the light. We are coming upon the last light. I don't want to miss the last light. It's—refreshing.

Would you like to know what I find refreshing?

I'd like that.

Silence.

I, also, am fond of silence.

Are you?

Quite.

Would you like to join me, then, in a moment of refreshment?

What—like a soda pop? Would you like a soda pop?

Will you join me, my good detective, would be another way to say it, in a moment of quiet contemplation?

Over a soda pop?

IN SILENCE.

Oh. Right. Quite right. Quite . . . quiet . . . quite quiet . . . kwy . . . it . . . it . . . It's a little ditty . . . a dirty little irksome ditty . . . dirty little ditty . . . diddy . . . Did he—did he sing a dirty little ditty . . . ? Did he sing a dirty little ditty in his dirty little dinghy . . . ? Did—did you know that apprentices in training to become sumo wrestlers are made to wipe the asses of their masters, given the prohibitive nature of the latter's greater girth?

I am engaged at present in a personal fantasy in which my hands are wrapped around your neck and squeezing.

Which is funny, when you think about it, because, in some small way, I am *your* apprentice.

I'm beginning to feel quite at home here.

It *is* comfortable.

I think maybe I'll sit down on the floor over here.

You're not feeling well?

I've lost the taste.

You're not hungry?

I'm out of the hunt.

What hunt?

Like you say, it's an expression.

You don't want to proceed?

I've lost the stomach.

Like the Mathematician?

. . . Essentially.

Is it my fault?

It's not about you.

Am I doing well?

You're doing fine.

Not well?

Fine.

. . . I rather thought I was doing well.

I think maybe I'll have a little nap.

You're going to sleep?

I might.

You'll miss the last light.

Detective?

Thank you for calling me that.

Do you think maybe he'll medicate us?

Who?

The doctor.

He's a *nice* man.

Perhaps we'll ask him.

You want I should fetch him?

We'll ask him when he comes.

If he comes.

We'll just lie here then.

Let's do that.

We'll ask him if he comes.

But I'm not—I just want to be up front about this—I'm not willing to do that for you—wipe your ass, I mean. Apprenticeship aside. Are you going to sleep? A man's got to draw the line, and I guess that

Night is falling.

this is where I draw mine . . . I think you're sleeping . . . Well, it's for the best . . . Night is falling . . . Though I guess I would, still, in an emergency. If your life was on the line. If you were, you know, all plugged up or something. Backed up. Irregular . . . I don't know . . . Is everything . . . settling in?

It all settles soundly.

You're awake.

I am.

I thought that you were sleeping.

I'm trying to.

Did I wake you?

No. I wasn't sleeping.

But you'd like to.

Yes.

Sleep.

. . .

Can I ask you something?

Anything. You can ask me anything.

How do you sleep?

. . . I'm afraid I don't understand the question.

I guess it's not so much a *how* as a *why*.

Why am I trying to sleep?

That's the question.

Everyone needs to sleep at one time or another.

I guess it's not so much a *how* or a *why* as a—

I keep wondering if I'll awake one morning with the resolve to live.

Ah.

. . .

You go ahead and sleep then. I'm going to stay up for the last, I think, light . . . still . . . I don't know how you do that though . . . Sleep, I mean . . . to go to sleep, I mean, with the knowledge that you are all that remains of the world . . . to go to sleep with the knowledge that you are all that remains of the world, and to know that you may never wake. Know what I mean?

. . .

You don't know what I mean.

. . .

I'll tell you what I mean.

. . . Quietly.

Sleep. When I am standing, as now, in the last light, and the last light recedes, it is as though it has consumed me, or, rather, it is as though I have consumed the light and this—*thing* occurs where I, like, I remove myself from myself and the light takes over, it takes *me* over, but—I'm not articulating very well here, it's—well, you might think I experience a loss of control, when I give over my control, but there's more to it than that, clearly, because it's not so much what I lose as what I gain, or rather not what I gain but where I go, where I. *Go*. I go places, man. I see things. I can see things that no one else can see. I love that crystal white safe place. Nothing can touch me, I am not any longer physically touch-able, if that makes sense, I am not even—I cannot even touch myself. I mean I can see myself as from outside of myself, I can see myself outside of *time* I can see myself *at all times* I can see myself at *all times present*—I can see myself, as now, as if it is a *now* and not a *then*, presenting the Mathematician with a mechanical series of truly bone-splitting blows with my strap and with my stick and with my bare fists and—oh boy um. It's otherworldly. I cannot feel my fists. I can hear his screams but only as from a great distance or as through a—distant aperture in an otherwise impenetrable canvas of clouds. An aperture or a tunnel. A tunnel bathed in light. I can see myself as at the end of a tunnel bathed in light. It's like I'm not there down there I mean I'm *there* but I'm not. There. It is the essence the *essence* it is the essence of *being* like I'm finally part of some thing that—some essential thing that—that composes me. I am out of control yes but I am *composed* of what controls me it's otherworldly it passes through me I am. *I am light*. Not light like heavy but a goddamned shimmering ray of light a point of light a *pinpoint* of light an accelerating cosmic particle warping and morphing with a boundless energy from a mysterious source inside of me that accumulates to a critical mass when—BANG—I explode in brilliant yellow and white concentric waves of light that expand from the center of my being and pass through him I pass through on what composes him for a moment I compose him because aren't we, also, electric?

ARENʼT WE, ESSENTIALLY, ELECTRIC?

. . .

I think thatʼs what I was trying to say.

. . .

Heʼs um in the meantime heʼs easily relenting his apocalyptic polemic and is engaged instead in pleading negotiations with his god or with his gods or with his. Mother and he doesnʼt know it at the time because I am inside of him but I can feel him I can feel his. Pain. I get the message on a molecular level. I can feel, once again, my fists. I can hear, once again, his *please god* his *stop god* his *please please stop god*. I have returned to myself again. I am myself again and . . . I see him . . . I see him lying there his blood and tears and his I think his piss and his shit and what frightens me what—*frightens* me is that I want to thank him . . . for bringing me there. To my crystal white safe place. I want to—reach into him, to consume the stuff of him I want to. Hold him . . . *May I,* I ask, *may I* hold *you?* . . . May I, may I ask, *hold* you? . . . Hold . . . Detective? Smith? Detective Smith? Are you sleeping, or . . . No. I think you must be sleeping . . . Judging from the smell.

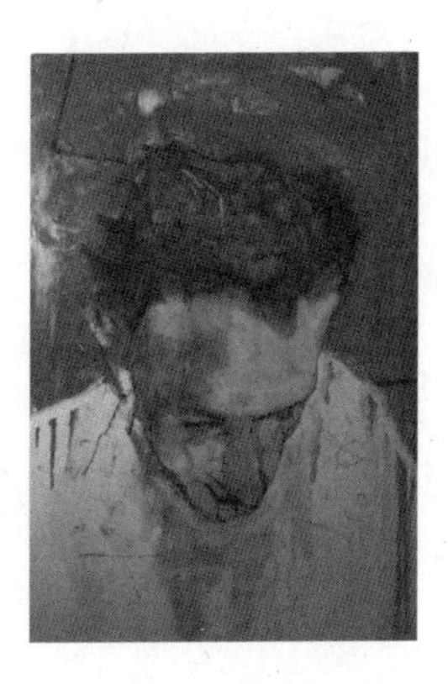

AARON PETROVICH is a writer of fiction and theatre living in Brooklyn. He is a regular contributor to the *Exquisite Corpse,* and associate editor at Akashic Books. His theatrical works have appeared in the Midtown International Theatre Festival, Manhattan Theatre Source, Improvised and Otherwise (a festival of sound and form), the Estrogenius Festival and the New York Solo Play Lab.

VILEM BENES was born in Zlin in the former Czechoslovakia. He moved as a young man to the U.S. with his family. He currently lives and paints in Brooklyn, New York.